FAITH RENEWED

DR. S. RADHAKRISHNAN

HIND POCKET BOOKS
A Penguin Random House Company

HIND POCKET BOOKS

USA | Canada | UK | Ireland | Australia
New Zealand | India | South Africa | China

Hind Pocket Books is part of the Penguin Random House group of companies
whose addresses can be found at www.hindpocketbooks.com

Published by Penguin Random House India Pvt. Ltd
7th Floor, Infinity Tower C, DLF Cyber City,
Gurgaon 122 002, Haryana, India

HIND
POCKET
BOOKS

First published in Hind Pocket Books by Penguin Random House India 2019

10 9 8 7 6 5 4 3 2 1

The views and opinions expressed in this book are the author's own and the facts are as reported by him which have been verified to the extent possible, and the publishers are not in any way liable for the same.

ISBN 9789353492601

Printed at Replika Press Pvt. Ltd, India

www.hindpocketbooks.com

HIND POCKET BOOKS

FAITH RENEWED

Dr. Sarvepalli Radhakrishnan was a philosopher, leader and most of all, an exemplary teacher. His achievements in these fields are remarkable. His first book 'The Ethics of The Vedanta and Its Material Presupposition', being his thesis for the M.A. degree examination, established his fame as a philosopher with an unquestionable ability. All his works were a landmark in their respective fields. There was a solid sense of social commitment in his work. He was awarded the Bharat Ratna in 1954, for his meritorious service to mankind. Among the many other honours he received were the British Knight Bachelor in 1931, and the commonwealth Order of Merit (1963), but ceased to use the title 'Sir', after India attained independence.

CONTENTS

Ishavasyam idam sarvam
yat kim cha jagatyam jagat
tena tyaktena bhunjitha, ma gridhah
kasyasvidhanam.

Isha Upanishad

FELLOWSHIP AND FREEDOM

It is the same atmosphere that you breathe in whatever part of the world you are, when you get into a university. In each generation, the universities have to reckon with the problems that face them. Our generation has its own specific problems to tackle. After the Second World War we have had the emergence of free nations in Asia and Africa. We have also what may be regarded as a revolution, a social revolution, of rising but yet unfulfilled expectations in the world. There is an increasing emphasis on science and technology, and emphasis which requires us to use the latest methods for the purpose of satisfying the legitimate aspirations of the submerged peoples of the world. And, above all, we have the great interest of peace.

After the end of the Second World War, a

number of nations in both Asia and Africa have become free. But political freedom is not an end in itself. We may have political freedom but if the people die of starvation, if they are ill-clad, ill-housed, ill-educated, if they suffer from destitution, disease, poverty, ignorance, then that freedom is not worth much. So, all over the world you have now a demand that the people of the world must be provided with the elementary necessaries of food, clothing and shelter, if their self-expression and development are not to be impeded. The only way by which we can set these things at rest is by the development of science and technology, the application of them to agriculture, industry, medicine, etc. These are the specific problems which face every university.

A university is called upon to train students for tackling these specific problems. You must send out men and women who are capable of teaching, who are capable of helping the industrialization or the modernization of the country, who are able to bring people together. They should consider themselves not be citizens of this or that nation, however much that may be necessary, but the citizens of the world as a whole.

The world requires to be treated as a unit. The methods of transport and communication, the way in which we are able to listen to the events which occur in distant parts of the world practically immediately — all these things make clear that the purpose of the world, the cosmic will, is for establishing, to use the words of the Holy Prophet, a family on earth. A family, a fellowship in which all members co-operate as equal units — it is that we are aiming at.

There are many people who think on account of their intoxication with the developments of science and technology that matter is the most important thing. But if we scrutinize a little further we will realize that these great developments of science and technology, if they establish anything, establish the omnipotence of the human spirit and not the omnipotence of matter. It is the human mind that sits in judgement on nature. Whether it is scientific discovery or technological development or artistic creation, the human being does not regard himself as a single item in a series of objective happenings. He believes that there is an element of subjectivity, an element of spirit in man which enables him to do the wonderful things which he is doing.

There are people who say that we have travelled round the world — the cosmonauts have gone over the world — but we have not encountered anything Divine; which reminds us of what the people of an earlier age said: "We dissected the human body and did not discover the soul." Other people said: "We searched the sky with a telescope but did not find God there." We must realize that the knowledge which we gain by the sense and by the intellect is not complete. There is a kind of knowledge where the human being feels that he is spiritual in character, and it is this spirit which enables him to sit in judgement on nature, to discover the secrets of nature, to unravel the mysteries of this world and to realize that there is something more than what meets the eye.

What is science? Science is the pursuit of truth. And what is truth? Truth is not something which you manufacture from out of the resources of your mind; it is the pursuit of something which is extramental, which is objective, which is there to which the human individual has to subscribe. All the great changes that have taken place from the time when men lived in primitive caves down to the time when we are trying to circle the earth, when we are trying to traverse regions of space — all these things are due not to mere mind or the senses but to that spirit of onward endeavour which is identified with what you call the spirit in man. When the scriptures declare that man is made in the image of God, or an Indian scripture says that *deba,* or body, is *devalaya,* or the dwelling of God, they are trying to tell us that whereas the cosmic happenings may take place, man is not to regard himself as mere item in the series of objective happenings. There is something in him which makes him sit in judgement on nature, which makes him understand what exactly it is that nature reveals. It is, therefore, necessary for us to realize that if we suppress the spirit in us, if we overlook the inwardness of the human being, we lapse into rigidity, we lapse into routine and we shall not be able to succeed in trying to understand nature or do anything.

What is art again? Artistic creation is something where you feel an experience and you impregnate that experience with your own personal spiritual intensity and make it come alive — that is what art means.

In our country, it is said, art is that which transmits to you a sense of the eternal, a sense which is beyond the merely temporal. A sense of something which is non-temporal in this world is conveyed to you by the achievements of the arts. Whether it is scientific creation or artistic endeavour or even a technological development, all these things make you feel that you are not merely a part of nature; in a larger sense there is a non-natural element in you, an element which exceeds mere nature; that element, therefore, is to be called the spirit in man. It is that spirit which is responsible for all the achievements which we have had in this world. It is not a thing which can be equated with mere mechanical nature. When people tell us that we are the victims of necessity, call it mechanical, providential or dialectical, they overlook the instinct for greatness and the instinct for freedom which are located in the heart of man. If we are merely the products of necessities, natural or providential, mechanical or dialectical, there will be no progress in this world at all. It is because there is something which is beyond the mechanism of the world that we are able to see that there is something universal.

Each human individual has to be a unique expression of that universal element; each human being is both unique and universal. He has in him an element of the Divine as also an element of nature. When the two things get integrated, then it is that you call a human being a fulfilled human being, a perfect human being, one who has been able to realize the discords and to overcome the discords to make of himself a single home.

When you say that here are these things, the spectacular development of nuclear physics, the arms which we have produced and which threaten us with ultimate destruction, you will note, on the other hand, that we also feel a biological instinct for survival. It is necessary for us to overcome the temptations of these nuclear developments, and we must try to establish supremacy over them. They are not our masters. We discovered nuclear weapons. We who discovered them can use them for peaceful purposes and need not use them for self-destruction or the annihilation of humanity.

Let us remember that in this world there have been many civilizations, one after the other — Babylon, Assyria, Greek. When you look into the history of those civilizations, you will discover one fundamental fact: those which laid the stress on matter, on weapons, on arms, have passed away. Those which laid their stress on the development of friendship, love, brotherhood, have survived. They may be in a very lethargic way; but all the same, they have survived.

If history has any lesson to teach us, it is this lesson: that nations which pledge themselves to peace and friendship, and which pledge themselves to use the greatest developments of science and technology for establishing human fellowship, it is such nations that have survived. And I have no doubt that in this age, when we are faced by annihilation or extension of human fellowship, we will adopt human fellowship, and overcome the obstacles which nuclear weapons set before us. Our doubt will be replaced by faith, our despair by hope, our uncertainty by conviction.

Man has the tendency in him to overcome the evil. Every time we are faced by the duality of good and evil in human nature, we erect wonderful monuments for humanitarian work — the Red Cross, the Red Crescent and such other organizations. On the other hand, we develop too many weapons by which we inflict injury on man. We build up our defence forces; we also try to cure the evils which these defence forces cause to man. There is this duality, this dichotomy in human nature, this conflict between good and evil. There is this polarity, so to say, in human beings; it is this polarity that we have overcome. We have to see to it that evil is surmounted and good becomes successful. It is for this endeavour that human beings were created in this world. Whereas the sub-human species acts instinctively, automatically, the human species is expected to act with deliberate, conscious effort — this is what it is expected to do. And if we are to use wisdom for the purpose of overcoming the present catastrophic changes which threaten us, we have to overcome knowledge by wisdom.

It is wrong to think that science and religion are opposed to each other. Science and religion represent two dimensions to the human being, the rational and the spiritual. These two things cannot be divorced from each other; they must be co-ordinated, they must be integrated, they must be correlated, if a human being is to become really a human being. There is no conflict at all between the great developments of science and technology which we have and the true religious sense of wisdom which is essential for using these great instruments for the purpose of human welfare.

Human well-being is the end which we have to set before ourselves. Humanity is above all nations and we have to bring together the nations into a kind of fellowship. Just as human individuals have given up their right of private violence, as tribes have given up their private army, as they have concentrated all force in the hands of nation-states, and when disputes arise among individuals or tribes, they turn to the nation-states to adjudicate and execute justice, even so we will move forward to a time when nations will deprive themselves of a part of their sovereignty, deprive themselves of their arms and concentrate in a world authority all the forces of coercion which are available in the world and turn to that organization for the adjudication of problems and the execution of justice.

That is how historical development is taking place.

Creative Life

God is not somewhere up above us, He is the inner-most Being of one's own self, wrapped up, so to say, in so many covers or layers. If we are to discover the Universal within us, we have to detach ourselves, abstract it from the layers of body, mind and intellect, and see the Universal dwelling in each one of us. To get into touch with that Universal Spirit it means the fulfilment of man's being.

Man, as he is, is incomplete, ignorant, unregenerate, and he wishes to complete himself, to get beyond his present imperfections; and he tries to achieve completeness of being. That is possible only by vigorous discipline of mind, by developing chastity of spirit which does not recognize boundaries of nations, races, etc. And if we are able to attain to that kind of perfectness of being, completeness of being, we try to use that wisdom for the purpose of creating a better life in this world.

I may illustrate this by a reference to our flag, where you see the circle, the wheel of time that is perpetually moving. But it is not a cyclical movement, it is a spiral movement, ever advancing from one stage to another, from minerals to plants, plants to animals, animals to human beings, and human beings to God in man. So the wheel of time is represented by the circle. But does it rest on itself? Is time self-maintained, is it self-supporting, or does it depend on an eternal background and can we give any description of it? The answer again is the pure white background, what we call the white radiance of eternity. You cannot describe it. Any account you give of it falls short of its immense wealth. Therefore, the only homage which you can pay to it is the homage of adoration, of mere science: that is, the homage which the finite mind can pay to the infinite mystery which inspires the whole temporal process. So we put the white background there to give people a description of the Divine in halting words.

Logical propositions fall short of the wealth of that Being. Therefore, we say, "Do not quarrel about the names you give to the Divine, or about the way you take to the Divine. The ways may turn and twist but when you reach the top you witness the same spiritual landscape and from different parts of the world you beckon to those who are able to realize that."

If the temporal process, of which we are a part, is there, and if this temporal process rests on an eternal background, how can human beings find out how to live in the world of time with the perspective of eternity? It is not possible without incurring much sacrifice and cost. In our country, tapas, the burning of your appetites, the burning of your lower passions, the making of yourself a clean man, depends on fervour, austerity. It is the burning of the dross that is represented by the orange colour which we put at the top. So we have the wheel of time, the background of eternity and the discipline of suffering by which man can make himself live in this world with that final consummation, is that an end in itself? No, your whole attempt should be, when once you become disciplined, to produce creative life in this world. Creative life is always indicated by green colour. It is the colour of vegetation, it is the colour of all growth. So, we have in that flag a symbol of the universal process through which humanity has to go.

Live in the world of time, have the perspective of the eternal, discipline yourself so that in every act you do, you do it as a dedication to the eternal. And all your activities are to be utilized for the purpose of producing a better life, a creative life, in which every man will have more amplitude of existence, more richness of being, more fervour of friendship. That is what our flag stands for, and it is that which constitutes the final goal of humanity, when we rise from our present existence to a better life.

House of Knowledge

In every university the library occupies a prominent position. The Bodleian Library at Oxford, the British Museum Reading-Room of London, the Cambridge University Library, the Library of Congress aspirants go for study, reflection and research. You will be surprised to learn, but it is true, that many of the greatest writers of our time, people who moulded the thought of our country, were students all their lives, pursuing their studies in libraries. Bernard Shaw and Karl Marx were regular visitors to the British Museum Reading-Room.

So, if a university has to fulfil its very important function the library occupies a prominent place. Unfortunately today many of our young students are content with merely reading the notes which their professors give them. They have neither the time nor the inclination to read great books. Nothing opens out a man's mind, broadens his horizon, as reading the great classics. I would advise everyone, not merely students but ourselves, the leaders of our country, to spend some time every day in the study of the classic, take their thoughts away from the hurly-burly of politics, from the rough and tumble where we are lost in excitement and passion. We must be in a position to decide all issues with calmness, with composure and with judgement. For that, there can be no greater preparation than an hour of study of the great classics.

A classic is strictly a contemporary work. It is meant for all generations. It is not meant merely for the time in which it is written. When you open a classic, you will find there a sense of discrimination, a sense of judgement. You yourself grow, you are endowed with new eyes with which to look at the world. That is the true purpose of a classic.

One of our popular verses says: *samsara visha vrkshasya dve phale amurtopame kavyamurta rasasvadah samlapah sajjanaihsaha.* In this poison tree of *samsara,* there are two fruits of inestimable value which have nectar-like quality: the tasting of the flavour of the classics and communion with great men. A university must bring the two together, must house the classics; must also collect men of greatness of spirit so that the students by their study of the classics and communion with the great professors, great celebrities who are brought together, get truly educated and civilized so far as their behaviour is concerned. Anger, greed and jealousy are the baser side of our nature. These are things which we have to control. We can control them effectively and efficiently by the study of these things.

It is not necessary for us to think that science gives us this, art gives us that, literature gives us a third. The house of knowledge cannot be divided against itself. It is one indivisible whole. It is a particular spiritual direction — *prayojanam tatva darshanam* — of the *shastras.* All the sciences enable us to probe a little into the mystery of reality. Science is imaginative adventure, it is an adventure of the human mind to understand a little more of the mysteries that surround us. So also is literature: it gives us moral insight; it enables us to know the feeling and passions of men; it tells us what we should avoid, what we should not.

A great writer, Thucydides, writing about the Peloponnesian War, tells us that love of power is the most wicked harlot in the world which seduces great men and great nations and brings them down to their ruin. He warns us against the seductive nature of love of power and he tells us that if we succumb to its temptations, great men and great nations, both succumb, both fall down, both become prostrate. So it is that we should discover from these great classics that what builds up a nation are the good qualities of humanity, fellowship and compassion; that what destroys a nation are hatred, greed, suspicion and jealousy of one another, Fellowship makes for life; lack of fellowship makes for death. If we understand these things which we have in our classics, we will be true students of a university.

In every individual you have chords of fortitude, heroism, passion and the capacity to lay down his life for an abstract idea or a great cause. If we appeal to our young men and women to sacrifice themselves for a great cause, there will be adequate response. While the students and the young men are able to give us that kind of response, we must also give them the right kind of leadership. If we have both great leadership and great service, the sense of service and devotion to a cause, I have no doubt that our country will become a great one. I am optimistic. We have seen our country pass through several vicissitudes; it has passed through several chances and changes. For over four to five thousand years, by its great capacity for self-renewal, by adoption of penetrating vision and the practice of love and compassion, we have been able to sustain this country. It will be sustained hereafter also because I know that deep down in human nature there is this readiness to respond to any kind of great call, readiness to take risks, readiness to lay down one's life. We will not be unworthy of this popular, spontaneous, great enthusiasm that we find all over the country, if we mobilize it, canalize it and use it for the purpose of building up a great world.

PRIMACY OF HUMAN INDIVIDUAL

You have in the *Gita* a saying, *jnanam vijnana sahitam*. Philosophic wisdom and scientific knowledge should go together. There is no distinction so far as the purpose is concerned between sciences and arts — *sarvashastra prajnanam tatva darshanam*. Every science has for its ultimate aim nothing more than an insight into reality, the understanding of the nature of the world and the universe. That happens to be the goal of all *shastras*.

People who are educated should have discipline, devotion and dedication, qualities lacking in our country at the present moment. We are trying to put our self-interest higher than the national interest. Our particular fashions and fads, our prepossessions, are the things which obsess us, and we seem to forget the larger need of developing this country.

You talk about Gandhiji and Nehru, the former emphasizing philosophic truth, the latter emphasizing technology. These are not mutually exclusive, these go together. Every science develops in you the quality of dedication, discipline and the removal of personal preferences. Every art gives you an insight into reality. So, there is not much distinction between the two. But now in our country, we are trying to develop a secularist, socialist, democratic society.

Secularism does not mean the neglect of religion. It means respect for all religions. One of the great Sikh Gurus said: *mandir masjid tere dham, ishvara allah tere nam*. It clearly shows that the same God dwells in temple and mosque; the same God is addressed by the different names of Isvara and Allah. Secularism, let it be clearly understood, is not neglect of religion; it is not indifference to religion, but respect for all faiths, respect for everything which a human being holds sacred.

When you talk of a socialist society, the

meaning of socialism is merely this : the greatest problem, the greatest challenge to our country today is the colossal poverty in which our people live. By industrial and economic development, we are trying to increase our wealth, but we want to see to it that this increased wealth is equitably distributed, is not confined to a limited few but that the ordinary people get the results of increased production, agricultural and industrial. If national wealth increases, the individual's wealth also should increase. We should see to it that the increase in wealth is equitably distributed.

We believe in a democratic society, a society which asserts the freedom of the human spirit. What is the good of earning the whole world if we lose our own soul, the primacy of the human individual, the dignity of the human spirit? We are trying to work out our Constitution within the limits of a democratic framework. We do not wish to use coercion, we do not wish to use methods including terror, we do not wish to adopt intimidation. We do not believe in indoctrination. We believe in enabling each individual to seek the truth and find out for himself without any kind of interference from outsiders. That is the meaning of democracy.

The meaning of eduction is to emancipate the individual. By means of eduction, you get the life eternal, you get freedom. Jesus Christ tells us, "ye shall know the truth, the truth shall make you free." The meaning of it is: free yourself from prejudices, from superstitions, from all allegiance to caste and community. See that you are a human being first and foremost, and let your sympathy extend to all objects of humanity. Wherever there is a human being in suffering or in trouble, it is your duty to go to his succour. If you are a truly good soul, if you are a truly educated individual, if you are truly emancipated, the suffering of every individual in this world will hurt you as if it were your own suffering. Your heart should become as naked as a nerve itself, and it must respond to the sufferings of other people. That is what we mean by education.

Education must make you civil in your behaviour. You must be stern with yourself but

be charitable to others. Whatever faults you have, try to correct them. But so far as other people are concerned, try to understand the position in which they happen to be and be charitable. Do not have malice. Do not adopt ideas that you are the superior and that others are inferiors. If you were in their position, you would not have done much better; that idea must enter your mind. So, the aim of education is to be severe with yourself but charitable to others.

Inner Life

I listened with great attention to the prayers which were recited by the representatives of different religions. You see there one basic quality. You see the quality of the potential divinity of man. The four Vedas have emphasized the potential spirituality of every human being. The Christian prayer spoke of the immortal heritage of which we are the inheritors. We are the children of immortality. The Buddha tells us that *maha karuna chittam* is to be found in every human individual. The Muslim prayer looks upon God as the Merciful, the Compassionate.

A Muslim saint said that we are born once from the womb; we are born a second time through our own self-knowledge. Almost all the prayers talk about the need for the deepening of one's awareness and extending one's object of compassion. We all are talking about these things; but there is very little practice to bring to a realization this spiritual character of man. We live on the surface. We do not know what we want, and we do not want what we know.

Our life is nothing more than a succession of sensations: we pass from one thing to another. I saw a room dedicated to meditation. I asked myself how many people do meditate truly? I asked one of my most illustrious friends to meditate for a little while, and he told me, "When I shut my eyes, I see newspapers coming up before me and anecdotes pass through my mind".

To have the capacity to concentrate your mind on one single purpose is not a thing which you can have easily. It requires great practice, great concentration. Even for a little thing we do require it. Absolute attention is complete prayer. If you are able to attend to any one thing completely, concentratedly, that is the highest kind of prayer that you can submit to the Divine.

Most of us pass out of this world without recognizing that spiritual possibility in us. That has been the misfortune of this world today. Great intellectuals that we are, we are able to do wonderful things; but have we explored the possibilities of our inner life? Have we been able to understand what it is that distinguishes us from the animal creation? What it is that makes a human being a human being? Solitude, capacity to meditate, capacity to concentrate — these are the things which are essential.

For the cultured mind, there is one goal and all activities are turned towards the attainment of that goal. For an uncultured mind, it is many-branched, endless. If we are to get all these things to converge on one single root, on one single path, what is essential is this kind of devotion to the Supreme. By love of God, you get detached from the rest of the world. If you want to develop *vairagya* or dispassion, the first essential is that you should have *anuraga* or passionate concern for the Supreme. That is what you are expected to do. We do not have it. We are neurotic, unstable, hysterical; we want to take sedatives to go to sleep, and we require a stimulant to get up from our beds. That is the position in which we are.

Recently I was on a visit to the United State of America. A set of young men and women came up to me and asked me, "What is wrong with us?" I said, "There is nothing wrong with you? Why do you assume there is anything wrong with you?" They replied, "No Sir, do not flatter us; there is something wrong with us." I told them, "Well, if you insist, I am telling you something. Your Founding Fathers came to this country; they had abounding faith and they had the pioneering spirit. Their pioneering spirit enabled them to develop amazing economic prosperity. There is a danger that in this prosperity you might lose an abiding faith which you also have. I do not say you have lost it. I say there is a danger of your losing it." Why is it that in affluent societies, where people have everything to eat and drink, we have the largest number of suicides? Man does not live by wealth alone. The Upanisads say that. Not by means of wealth can a man fulfil himself. He requires other dimensions which he has to develop. If he does not develop them, he dies an unfulfilled being. In the midst of plenty, he suffers from spiritual poverty. It is that spiritual poverty that has led times without number to lives of frustration and made people even give up their lives. That is why it is essential for us to remember all that these prayers have brought to our attention, that is, that a man's life should get into the dimension of depth. If you are able to do anything with a sense of seriousness, earnestness and purposefulness you will be happy. But if you do it merely because you have to do it, you are unhappy. We are perpetually turning between the good and the pleasant. We prefer the pleasant to what is good for us. Hence there is suffering.

If this world is to be retrieved, an essential thing is the development of this art of meditation, of cleansing ourselves, of the churning of our minds and allowing our deepest passions to come out to face them clearly, austerely.

There is a world of difference between loneliness and solitude. Most of us are lonely in a crowd. But when we are alone we are not solitary because we have an eternal companion by our side. Whatever activity we indulge in, the eternal companion is there, the perpetual friend is present there. If we are not able to recognize this thing, we may be in a crowd and we may feel lonely; we may be alone and yet feel more or less sociable in our character. Compassion is the necessary quality of this deepest awareness. If we recognize that every human being has a spark of the divine, if we know that he has this element, that the invisible arms of the divine are supporting him even when he does the most atrocious crime, we will never judge another harshly. Deepen your awareness and extend your objects of compassion. If you are able to do that, you are truly a human being.

My friend Shrimati Rukmini Devi said that art is something which elevates. When does it elevate? It does not elevate by merely touching your senses, when it merely instructs your mind. But when it touches your depth, when it is able to devastate your being, gives you new eyes with which you are able to see a new world, if you are able to do that, then art elevates. It is deep calling to the deep.

Kalidasa, replying to a question about why a painting was not authentic, said that meditation or concentration had become impaired. The painter had not been full of concentration and his attention had wandered; therefore, the painting itself had failed. So *samadhi* or concentration, is essential not merely for the production of great literature or the production of great art, but for the production of greatness in everything, whether in scientific discovery, technological device, literary production, or artistic excellence.

Man must throw himself completely into the object; he must be able to impregnate what he sees with the intensity of his own experience. He must be able to feel, he must drown himself out there. That is ecstasy. Unless you are able to get that kind of feeling, you will never produce great art. It is when the deep calls to the deep that there is transformation of your whole being. It is that transformation Shrimati Rukmini Devi had in her mind when she spoke about the spiritual quality of art. Art ennobles, it lifts you up, makes you a different being and art is something which we should cultivate.

Reverence For Life

Tapas is mental travail. Panini tells *tapa alochana,* deep self-reflection; by *alochana* or reflecting on the facts of experience and not being satisfied with first appearances, is any kind of progress made. If science does not advance in research, it grows stagnant and dies. It is, therefore, very essential that those who are dealing with the medical sciences should do their utmost to keep the flame burning brighter and yet brighter as the generations pass.

We have in our country a very great tradition of not merely reverence for life but reverence for suffering, reverence which made us take to healing people. The *ayurvedic* science says: *rogah, roga-hetuh, roganivrttih arogyam.* Buddha followed with *duhkha, duhkhahetuh, dukhanivrttih nirvanam. This* kind of analysis of human suffering has been there. The greatest of our seers were people who tried to help those that needed comfort, who tried to heal sickness, tried to cure the blind, and tried to make the lame walk. That is what great people have said and done in their own lives.

Therefore, this medical profession is a profession of the greatness humanity, of the greatest service. If anyone carries on research here, it will be applied not merely to his own country or to his people but to the whole world. When Madame Curie, a Pole settled in France, discovered radium, it was not merely for the Poles or for the French but for the whole world that she had discovered it.

We have been doing our utmost since Independence, by increasing facilities for medical education, upgrading several institutions and instituting post-graduate sections in different branches of study. But to a real medical revolution which is taking place today all over the world, I do not think that we have contributed in a very significant way.

If you wish to have research, you require

certain conditions. You require men of talent, you require an atmosphere and environment, you require the tools and the equipment. These things are essential. I do not see why, with the increasing facilities which we now have, there should be any lack of these.

Our boys and girls, our men and women, are not inferior in intelligence or innate ability. They are people who can be raised to the level of first-class researchers in medical science, as they have been raised in other sciences in this country. Tools and equipment may be costly and expensive, but even then we are spending much money on so many things; and I do not see any reason why we should not provide our people with the right equipment and tools.

We need also the environment, an atmosphere of research and love for advancing the frontiers of knowledge. This must be instilled into every young man. There is no use in bulldozing human minds. We must try to give the critical and creative powers with which we are endowed full scope and opportunity for expression. I think that if our teachers have that sense of not merely transmitting knowledge but transmitting love of research, our boys and girls will respond duly.

Even today we hear of many cases of cholera in some parts of our country, a disease which has been wiped out in many advanced countries. It does not depend merely on medical science, it depends on the raising of environmental hygiene, sanitation and proper water supply.

You find also that heart aliments are on the increase. That again is owing to the lack of some kind of tranquillity in the human being who faces the stress and storm of life. The strain through which we are passing makes us feel worried, and worry is one of the greatest causes of any kind of heart trouble.

We find mental illness also on the increase. It is owing to the fact that the human being has reduced himself in many cases to a mere reactor to the changes which take place in his environment. He does not exercise his critical and creative faculties in accepting the challenges and overcoming them. Man should not be reduced to the position of a mere robot; he must not become an automaton. He is not merely a cog in the wheel; he is one who has been responsible for all the achievements which we have made since the beginning of history. It is the free spirit of man that can sit in judgement on the environment, penetrate its secrets, mould the environment to suit his pattern, his own desire. So, the free spirit of man must not be curbed.

It is Jung, the great psychiatrist, who said that sixty per cent of the mental cases which came to him were due to lack of faith, lack of purpose in life, to a certain vacuity, emptiness in the human being. The moment you give him faith, you give him a purpose in life, his mental disorder subsides.

It is known that we are born in this world to live for a great cause, to live for some supreme purpose. If we overlook that purpose, if we make ourselves an object in a series of happenings and do not make ourselves a subject of creativity, if we overlook that fundamental fact, then we will make ourselves subject to every kind of disorder.

So the one great thing necessary is to instil into our young men a purpose in life, a sense of dedication, and to make them feel that they are born in this life to do something great. That is what is necessary. Thc disruption of human relationships, which brings about so many casualties in this world, will all be overcome if man has love.

"I never met a man whom I did not like," said one of the great thinkers, "every man whom I met I liked until he disappointed me, until he made me to feel that there was something wrong which had to be set right." It is that passion, that passion for human relationships, the enlargement of human relationships, making people believe that we look upon them as something intelligent, dignified, which requires to be given every kind of attention. That will bring down cases of mental illness, and it will also bring down causes which break up human relationships with so much consequent tragedy.

The Ramayana and Indian Culture

This book, *Ramayana Katha* by Shri Raghunath Singh, Member of Parliament, will give our youth an idea about the fundamentals of our culture. At a time when great stress is properly laid in our schools and colleges on the study of sciences, pure and applied, we should not overlook the significance of a study of our ancient classics. All great thinkers ask us to know the self — *atmanam viddhi. The* classics are the chief means by which man learns about himself, his achievements and his failures, his powers and his limitations.

Indians are natural catholics, not in the religious but in the larger sense of being hospitable to other views and doctrines. They believe that religion consists in the vision of the Supreme and that it is transmitted by the impact of personality and not by the imparting of information. We must behold the truth and we become what we behold. If, in spite of the practice of religions all these centuries, we still live in a nightmare world, it is because we do not realize sufficiently that religion consists in the remaking of the self, in the refashioning of our nature and not in the repetition of hymns or observance of ceremonies. A strict discipline which integrates our nature is the demand of our age.

The forces which push men into conflicts are very deep-rooted and have characterized mankind throughout its existence. We should control these forces and subject them to discipline. Feelings and emotions are there in human nature breeding hatred and passions that have corrupted human life throughout history and do so still. On the other hand, there are inhuman nature cravings for beauty, moral aspirations, reverence for something greater than everything in the universe. These creative impulses give warmth and colour to life's fabric, its richness, fullness and diversity. But suddenly an impulse overtakes us and the higher impulses are suppressed and the more primitive ones come to the surface.

It is enough for the great teachers to proclaim the truth. It is for ordinary men to see the truth and apply it to their collective behaviour. It is the only way in which we can raise quality of our public judgement and conduct.

The *Ramayana Katha* recalls to our mind the perpetual conflict in human nature, the *devasura yuddha. God* and man are not separate from each other. The two are one substance made into two, *sattvam ekam dvidha krlam.*

The Ramayana is literature which makes for fellowship and reconciliation. It helps us to treat human beings with understanding and generosity. It sets forth the conscience of our people. Its lessons are of permanent value.

THE PROBLEMS OF EDUCATION

In the book, *The Education of the whole Man,* the well-known educationist of the United States, Mr. Ralph Borsodi, has asked us to take a fresh look at the problems of education. All systems of education aim at the education of the whole man, though in practice they lay undue emphasis on physical efficiency or intellectual alertness or spiritual poise. These are not exclusive of each other. They are essential ingredients of a true system of education.

The Upanisads tell us that we should aim at the play of life, *pranaramam*, the satisfaction of mind, *mana anandam,* and the fullness of tranquillity, *santi samrddham.* The sickness of our society can be traced to one-sided development of education.

All knowledge is indivisible. Science and

technology, literature and art, philosophy and religion are varied manifestations of the spirit of man. They do not contradict one another but complement one another. The spirit in man sits in judgement on nature, discovers its secrets and increases our knowledge of nature. In art and literature the same spirit deals with the moods and passions, the intense experience of the human individual, especially his inner being. The same spirit probes into the mystery of the world, tries to understand a little of it.

Science and technology are a dialogue of the human spirit with nature. Literature and art are a dialogue of the spirit with oneself. Philosophy and religion are a dialogue of the spirit with the supreme mystery which underlies the universe. When people speak of a conflict between science and religion, they do not appreciate the spiritual character of science and the rational character of religion. When properly understood, science and religion help each other.

In the name of science and rationalism many of our societies have broken off their connection with past tradition. Their lives have become rootless. We have to grow our roots again. We have to combine ancient tradition with modern knowledge. If we wish to have an open society, we should have open minds.

The human being, through a balanced education, should become a work of art capable of quality and beauty of its own apart from any practical purpose to which his skills and powers are put.

The development of the human individual makes for the uniqueness of the individual. This uniqueness contributes to the fellowship of human beings. It leads one to the creative realization of the unity of mankind. There is no contradiction between seeing the truth in solitude and engaging in human affairs.

Significance Of The Upanisads

Human progress is built on acts of faith. The acts of faith on which our civilization is based are to be found in the principal Upanisads. When we are now setting out on a new era in the life of our country, we must go to the Upanisads for inspiration. They contain the principles which have moulded our history from its earliest dawn. Where we have failed, our defeat is due to our infidelity to the teachings of the Upanisads. It is therefore essential for our generation to grasp the significance of the Upanisads and understand their relevance to our problems.

The texts of the Upanisads are not to be read simply. They are meant for meditation. Take, for example, the very first verse with which this book opens:

ishavasyam idam sarvam
yat kin ca jagatyam jagat
tena tyaktena bhunjitha, ma gridhah
kasyasvid dhanam.

(Know that) all this, whatever moves in this moving world, is enveloped by God. Therefore find your enjoyment in renunciation; do not covet what belongs to others.

It makes out that this world is a perpetual procession of events where everything supersedes another. But this passing show is not all. It is informed by the Supreme Spirit, enveloped by God. We should not look at the world merely from the outside as a succession of events but perceive beneath it the burning intensity of significance which penetrates the succession. Every occasion of the world is a means for transfiguring insight. By renouncing everything we become the lords of everything. When we feel that the whole universe is inhabited by God, we become one with the universe. In the words of Trahorne, 'the sea flows in our veins.... and the stars are our jewels.' When all things are perceived as sacred, there is no room for covetousness or self-assertion.

What Is Secularism ?

In the book, *Indian Nationhood and National Culture,* Dr. S. Abid Husain indicates the central characteristics of Indian culture as it has grown from its beginning to its present position. His presentation of the subject is marked by ability, vision and purpose. He argues that there has been a common spiritual outlook on life, to which various races and religions have made contributions. 'India's cultural history of several thousand years shows that the subtle but strong thread of unity which runs through the infinite multiplicity of her life, was not woven by stress or pressure of power groups but the vision of seers, the vigil of saints, the speculation of philosophers, and the imagination of poets and artists and that these are the only means which can be used to make this national unity wider, stronger and more lasting.'

It may appear somewhat strange that our Government should be a secular one while our culture is rooted in spiritual values. Secularism here does not mean irreligion or atheism or even stress on material comforts. It proclaims that it lays stress on the universality of spiritual values which may be attained by a variety of ways.

Religion is a transforming experience. It is not a theory of God. It is spiritual consciousness. Belief and conduct, rites and ceremonies, dogmas and authorities are subordinate to the art of self-discovery and contact with the Divine. When the individual withdraws his soul from all outward events, gathers himself together inwardly, strives with concentration, there breaks upon him an experience, sacred, strange, wondrous, which quickens within him, lays hold on him, becomes his very being. Even those who are the children of science and reason must submit to the fact of spiritual experience which is primary and positive. We may dispute theologies but we cannot deny facts. The fire of life in its visible burning compels assent, though not the fumbling speculations of smokers sitting around the fire. While realization is a fact, the theory of reality is an inference. There is a difference between contact with reality and opinion about it, between the mystery of godliness and belief in God. This is the meaning of a secular conception of the State though it is not generally understood.

This view is in consonance with the Indian tradition. The seer of the Rg Veda affirms that the Real is one while the learned speak of it variously. Asoka in his Rock Edict XII proclaims: 'One who reverences one's own religion and disparages that of another from devotion to one's own religion and to glorify it over all other religions does injure one's own religion most certainly. It is verily concord of religions that is meritorious.'

Centuries later Akbar affirms: 'The various religious communities are divine treasuries entrusted to us by God. We must love them as such. It should be our firm faith that every religion is blessed by Him. The Eternal King showers his favours on all men without distinction.' This very principle is incorporated in our Constitution which gives full freedom to all to profess and practise their religious beliefs and rites so long as they are not repugnant to our ethical sense. We recognize the common ground on which different religious traditions rest. This common ground belongs of right to all of us as it has its source in the Eternal.

The universality of fundamental ideas which historical studies and comparative religion demonstrate is the hope of the future. It makes for religious unity and understanding. It makes out that we are all members of the one Invisible Church of God though historically we may belong to this or that particular religious community.

BUDDHISM

In 1938, during the Sino-Japanese war, Gandhiji reminded a Japanese statesman that we should re-learn the message of the Buddha and deliver it to the world:

'Today it is being denied everywhere... I have no message to give you but this — that you must be true to your ancient heritage. The message is 2,500 years old, but it has not yet been truly lived.'

In this year when we are celebrating the 2,500th anniversary of the Buddha's *parinirvana,* it is good to have a simple, readable account of the story of the Buddha revealing the great heights to which human thought and feeling have risen in his life and work.

Religion, for the Indian mind, whether Hindu, Jain, or Buddhist, is an endeavour to raise oneself to a higher level of being by discipline, mental, moral and spiritual. Dr. N. Gangulee (author of *The Buddha and His Message)* who spent the last years of his life in the study and meditation on the problems of religious life, makes out how the Buddha was man among men, a humanist interested in the perennial problem of how man can liberate himself from the shackles of mortality. We are caught in the wheel of time because we are not yet what we ought to become. If we are to be redeemed from time, we must practise self-discipline. By fasting and meditation, by silence and chastity, we dissociate the self from the automatism of habit. We break our bondage to the life of routine.

To break bonds is to taste freedom. It is to put away from us what is not ours. It is to realize that there is something unborn, *ajanta*, unbecome, *abhuta,* unmade, *akata,* uncomposite, *asamkhata,* undying, *amata,* which is the opposite of the flux or becoming.

> Change and decay in all around I see
> O Thou who changest not.

The Buddha calls himself *brahma-bhuta*, one who has become Brahman. When we are anchored in this wisdom, pride hatred and hypocrisy fall away. We are tolerant with the intolerant, gentle with the violent, detached from things in the midst of those who are attached to them.

Creeds and ceremonies, rites and rituals are there to help us to discover the divine in us. They are means to the end of spiritual life and quarrels about them are meaningless. The truly religious man is a reconciling spirit, who has a realization of the universality of the ultimate truth proclaimed by different faiths. Each one can preserve his own form of faith and yet grow by assimilating whatever is of value in other faiths so long as they are not spiritually incompatible with one's own. This is the law of spiritual growth.

The Buddha asks us to abandon the feeling of pride or superiority in matters of faith. Non-egoism, *anahamkara* is the need of both individuals and nations. Humility is the one thing lacking in the self-righteous crusading spirits of our time.

Let us learn to look upon the whole world as our own. No one is a stranger; nothing human is alien. "Do not deceive each other, do not despise anybody anywhere, never in anger wish anyone to suffer through your body, words or thoughts. Like a mother guarding her only son with her own life, keep thy immeasurable loving thought for all creatures. Above thee, below thee, on all sides of thee, keep on all the world thy sympathy and immeasurable loving thought, without any wish to injure, without enmity." —*Sutta Nipata.*

Message Of The Buddha

The teaching of the prophets is generally distorted by beliefs of the world and the interpretations of the priests. If we wish to ascertain what the founders of great religions thought, we have to get back to the original sources.

Buddhism in all its forms goes back to the life and 50 teachings of the Buddha. While the austerities practised by him till he attained enlightenment appeal to the Hinayana, the Pali, or the Southern school, his life of service and compassion for forty-five years after the attainment of enlightenment is the authority for the Mahayana, the Sanskrit, or the Northern school.

The religious quest springs from the consciousness of the imperfection and suffering of the world. The questions which worried Tolstoy in the fiftieth year of his life disturb all thinking men. 'What is life? What should I live for? Why should I do anything? Is there any meaning in life that can overcome inevitable death?' Nijinzky summed up the whole problem in his diary when he wrote: 'The whole life of my wife and of all mankind is death.' How can we be saved from the body of this death? This is the problem of religion.

The Buddha traces suffering to selfish desire. Suffering is the result of tension between a living creature's essential impulse to try to make itself into the centre of the universe and its essential dependence on the rest of creation. Craving is that which binds the individual to the creative process. The individual with selfish desire becomes the slave of the universe. We can overcome suffering only if we get rid of *trishna* or *tancha.* To attempt to get rid of suffering through the various devices of self-deception is not to cease to suffer but to suffer in a different way.

The Buddha formulates the eight-fold path of morality which helps us to eliminate selfish desire and overcome suffering. When the

Upanisads declare, 'That thou art, *tat tvam asi,* it is not a mere statement of fact. It is a call to action. Make thyself that which thou knowest thou canst be. Whereas the Hindu mind believes in a permanent element in the individual which can stand firm and unshaken in the midst of change, the Buddhist stresses the dynamic character of the self. No change is possible with an unchanging consciousness. We can achieve the possibilities in us by the exertion of the will rather than by the play of the intellect.

Religion is not a creed but a vital process. It is no use railing against God or destiny when we are ourselves the authors of our disgrace. If few are chosen it is because few choose to be chosen. The Buddha laid stress on the creative freedom of man. The Buddha did not encourage dependence on the supernatural. He could not conceive of being capable of creating a world for the express purpose of its creatures praising him. The ten *veramanis* or prohibitions or abstinences called *dasaila* or *dasasiksapada* which the novices in the path of Buddhism utter are given in these words: 'I take upon myself the abstinence,

(1) from destroying life,
(2) from taking what is not given,
(3) from leading an unchaste life,
(4) from speaking untruth,
(5) from giving myself to intoxicating drugs,
(6) from eating at irregular hours,
(7) from seeing musical and dancing performances and other shows and pageants,
(8) from wearing garlands, perfumes, unguents and other bodily decorations,
(9) from using high couches and seats,
(10) from accepting gifts of gold and silver.

The first five are the Buddhist *panchasila*.

panatipata veramani sikkha-padam samadiyami

adinnadana veramani sikkha-padam samadiyami

kamesu nicchacara veramani sikkha-padam samadiyam

musavada veramani sikkha-padam samadiyami

Sura-merayamajja-pamadatthana veramani sikkhapadam samadiyami.

Conflicts in the world are conflicts in the human soul enlarged. If men were at peace within themselves, the outer conflicts between nations would inevitably cease. By practising the Buddha's *Panchasila,* we will develop patience, courage, love and unselfishness. The Buddha teaches us that even in an age of anxiety and violence, it is possible to gain and maintain inner harmony, which is not at the mercy of outward circumstance.

Nirvanam paramam sukham. Nirvana is the highest bliss. It is not a negative state of annihilation, but a positive state of joy; consciousness grows from an unhappy to a beatific one. The Buddha does not tell us that man is but a bubble on the turbulent surface of nature and that he has no destiny save to undergo dissolution.

The Hindu affirms that man can realize his identity with Brahman, the ground of all being; the Buddhist says that man can live in a transfigured world where samsara and nirvana are one. In the *Mahasaccaka Sutta,* the Buddha himself is reported to have described the supreme triumph of reaching the goal of his quest as follows:

> When this knowledge, this insight, had arisen within me, my heart was set free from intoxication of lusts, set free from the intoxication of beco-mings, set free from the intoxication of ignorance. In me thus emancipated, there arose the certainty of that emancipation. And I came to know: 'Rebirth is at an end. The higher life has been fulfilled. What had to be done has been accomplished. After this present life, there is no further for this or that.' This last insight did I attain to is the last watch of the night. Ignorance was beaten down, insight arose, darkness was destroyed, the light came, in as much as I was there, strenuous, earnest, master of myself. Thus ended the struggle of six long years.

The Buddha is said to be a physician. Even as the physician strives to restore to health a sick man, the Buddha tries to restore us to our normal condition. If our leaders become normal, we may be able to replace the present social order in which division, falsehood and violence prevail, by a new one in which humanity, truth and brotherhood will reign.

On the occasion of the 2,500th anniversary of the Buddha's *parinirvana*, the Government of India decided to publish standard versions in the Devanagari script of the Pali and Sanskrit texts of the two schools, Southern and Northern, in the hope that some of the readers of these books may be impelled to love the good, to practise altruism and hold their spirit aloof from the desires and ambitions of the world.

Need For A Renewal Of Faith

The Third Five-Year Plan has just been published. It takes account of our achievements and failures in the last ten years in the different fields of agriculture, industry, education, health and housing, and sets forth the measures to be adopted to realize our social and economic objectives of larger employment and better opportunities for all.

Our country is growing better in many ways. Millions of our people are getting out of their ruts, out of their sheltered lives. There is an aspiration everywhere to improve the conditions of the lowly and the least fortunate. There is a yearning for greater understanding and goodwill among the people in the country. Yet there is a sense of disappointment. The old contempts and fears and the barriers of caste and community still divide us. They are undermining our democratic system which is based on the four principles of national unity, social justice, secularism which means respect for all faiths, and peaceful social change.

The social revolution now in progress has unleashed not unexpectedly destructive forces. These are the pains of the birth of a new order. Stability can be achieved only by carrying out the Directives laid down in the Constitution. Some of the social institutions which we uphold embody the principle of inequality. We invent empty excuses for our inaptitude in fighting social evils and breaking man's tyranny over man. All human beings, whatever their caste or community, race or religion, have a right to respect and friendship. Great patience and self-restraint are necessary if we are to weld together the different communities into a single whole.

To make a new India, we need not only industrial progress and political maturity, but also a renewal of faith in the future of our country. We must courageously scrap old loyalties which are out of date and build new institutions which are suited to modern conditions. Life is a constant adaptation to change. When different people meet together, it should not be the mere gathering of a crowd. There must be some bond of relationship if we are not to knock against one another. We must organize our emotions in terms of national unity. We cannot have national integration without national discipline, without national ethics. Decency in public life should be maintained. We need the dedicated efforts of all our citizens.

If we are divided in mind, we will be hesitant in action. Through panchayats, through schools and colleges, through the Press and the radio, through taluq boards and district councils, we should help our people to understand the scope and significance of our present venture in which all our nationals are participants. A nation is bound by past memories and hopes for its future. We have historical memories and national aspirations. Let us integrate the two and march forward to the goal of a civilized, democratic Welfare State.

SCIENCE AND THE MODERN WORLD

Science attempts to obtain a disinterested knowledge of the world of nature. In technology we use this knowledge for the manipulation of things. Under the stimulus of recent advances in scientific knowledge and technological devices, the pattern of life is changing at an unprecedented rate. The daily life of the people is being revolutionized. The people of Asia and Africa have now a vision of the possibility of the good life for all. They believe that science can liberate their lives from destitution and disease.

In advanced countries, life-expectancy has been raised, work-loads have been reduced; leisure for self-development for all people is not a remote ideal. We can help those who are physically, mentally and emotionally deficient. Man is struggling to shape himself anew that he may achieve his high destiny which life has shown can be his. The wonders of science, what it has done for us, what it will do for us, are a part of the picture.

Scientists have also created for us a period of tension, danger and opportunity. If other civilizations perished of creeping paralysis or of pernicious anaemia, ours may end, if it does, in convulsions. The new powers which science and technology have put into our hands have increased vastly our capacity for shaping our life for good or evil. If rightly used, these powers can give us strength, a fuller freedom and a better human life for the individual and society. If abused, they can bring about chaos and destruction. The present is a period of testing.

The scientist is a dedicated servant of truth. Because he deals with the world of nature, he is likely to overlook the role of the human spirit in scientific endeavour. If we believe that there is nothing more than the world of nature to which we are tied, we will suffer from an inner emptiness, anxiety, and split-consciousness. If we realize that it is the spirit of man that sits in judgement on nature, that penetrates into it and reveals its secrets, we will know that man is essentially a subject, a spark of the spirit and not a mere object, a thing among things. When this subjectivity is recognized, the distance between science and humanity is diminished.

The future is not inevitable. Even the materialists who believe that man is determined behave as though they had decisions to make and it is important that they decide rightly. In great crises we become conscious not only of our tenderness and compassion but of our fear, greed and hostility to others. Man, the subject, can control his inward distortions and shape the world to the pattern of his ideal.

The different manifestations of the human spirit form a coherent whole. Our intellectual house cannot be divided against itself. Knowledge is a unity. The different sciences and the subjects covered by the humanities are interconnected by relevance and meaning.

In this exciting age of science, our young

men and women should be given a balanced education. They should be taught the methods and achievements of the sciences, basic and applied, as well as literature, philosophy and history.

DEMOCRACY - A WAY OF LIFE

Democracy is not merely a form of government; it is a way of life, an act of faith in the dignity and freedom of the individual. Man is not a mere wisp of straw tossed about by the winds of nature or of history. Democracy is opposed to the view that holds that the life of each man and woman is completely determined by subhuman forces beyond the control or even the knowledge of either the individual or society. It holds that history is moved forward by men and ideas. Human beings are not to be treated as commodities to be bought and sold.

In the vastly standardized world, human beings seem to lose faith in themselves. Our vision should not be dimmed and our purposes should not be shaken by circumstances which seem to be forbidding. The advances of science and technology indicate the wondrous power of the mind of man, and a true democracy upholds the dignity of the human mind. John Milton says: "Know that to be free is the same thing as to be pious, to be wise, to be temperate and just, to be frugal and abstinent and lastly to be magnanimous and brave."

To make the world a better place to live in, we must do a better job of ourselves. Freedom is inward restraint. Adult franchise which we have adopted is an expression of our faith in the sanctity and freedom of the human individual.

A democratic form of government should function for the good of every person. We do not have a democratic form of government if a few individuals have privileges that are denied to others. By checks and balances, a democratic constitution prevents the concentration of power in a few people. Possession of power does not lead to humility but to conceit. Acton's words are well known: "Power tends to corrupt and absolute power corrupts absolutely." Acton quotes Leibnitz: "Those who have more power are liable to sin more; no theorem in geometry is more certain than this." Fenelon said: "Power is poison. It corrupts the conscience, hardens the heart and confounds the understanding." Those who have power need to exercise great vigilance.

Political freedom is not enough. No one can exercise his vote freely so long as he is a victim of hunger, poverty, illiteracy and exploitation. People require to be emancipated from a slavery far more cruel than chains and shackles. The obstacles to freedom require to be removed. The economic side of the democratic ideal is equally important. Democracy is not to be identified with status quo and vested interests. The awakening of our people from listless fatalism to self-awareness and even to self-assertion is a ground for hope.

Our people are no longer willing to accept passively the gross inequalities of wealth and opportunity. An equitable social economy can be achieved only by the deliberate direction and control of the production and distribution of wealth. We must adopt the maxim that the free development of each is the condition for the free development of all. We must ensure and improve the welfare of the poorest classes without endangering the spiritual heritage which gives dignity to the life of man.

We must organize our economic life on the principles of political freedom and economic opportunity for all. We have adopted a mixed economy where the State undertakes enterprises which are too large for private enterprise.

When we do not have an educated electorate, a few leaders manipulate votes and adopt the methods of mass psychology. The responsibility of the leaders in a democratic constitution is great. Gandhiji tells us: "Those who claim to lead the masses must resolutely refuse to be led by them if we want to avoid mob law and desire ordered progress for the country. I believe that mere protestation of one's opinion and surrender to mass opinion is not only not enough, but in matters of vital importance, leaders must act contrary to mass opinion if it does not commend itself to their reason."

Fraternity, fellowship among nations, is one

of our directives. Science has created one world and a world community is the goal of human enterprise on earth. We live near the frontier that divides the old from the new. It was said of Pericles that he was a good Athenian but a bad Greek. He did not help to weld the Greek States into a nation.

Today nationalism has become out of date. It has become a force for disunity. It is efficient and valuable within a society but is not the ultimate principle of human behaviour. An unrestricted development of different nations, speaking different languages, following different laws and customs and seeking divergent ends will reduce the world to a babel of people. Nationalism is inadequate and, in the modern age self-destructive. It is a form of mass egotism and self-idolatry. Even nation-states have to admit a law higher than their own laws. Gandhiji said that his love of the Indian nation was different from the usual chauvinism. "My idea of nationalism," he said, "is that my country may become free; that, if need be, the whole country may die, so that the human race may live." None of the differences separating the governments of the world are as important as our membership of the human family.

Other countries revere as heroes those who believe in force as the only means for solving social and economic problems. They liberate their countries from political subjection by military methods. In India we revere as heroes those who believe in peace and use peaceful methods for the liberation of the country and for promoting social progress and solidarity among the people. Gandhiji's movement is of a piece with the Indian tradition which has established the empire of the spirit over a large part of Asia, an empire which is more enduring than what material power can achieve.

The greatest era of human history on earth is within our reach. There is no area that cannot be made habitable or fertile, no disease that cannot be conquered. We have only to rediscover our moral strength and redefine our purposes. No nation can prosper unless all prosper. This is the lesson of the diminished world, the shrunken globe. This is the price not of prosperity but of survival.

The working of parliamentary institutions helps us to acquire the qualities of humility, of tolerance. In short, it is an education in human decency.

Fulfilment Of Man

Philosophy has been the special subject of my own study, and there again I read in my student days many works of your professors. We had A. S. Pringle-Pattison, James Ward, and later Norman Kemp Smith and A. E. Taylor to study. Their works were textbooks for us when we were doing our Master of Arts course. And in English literature we had to read Scott's *The Bride of Lammermoor*. This gave us an idea of the romantic life in Scotland. It is no wonder that you have now these international festivals of music and drama as also a film festival. Many of our young men and women, I have no doubt, have greatly profited by these events.

The influence of Scottish philosophy in general has been very considerable but not always good. There are people today who profess a doctrine called logical positivism and claim philosophical descent from David Hume. They tell us that this doctrine as a form of knowledge consists of matters of fact and relations of ideas. If there is a book on divinity or metaphysics which deals with anything less, I shall dismiss it as sheer sophistry and illusion — these are the sort of words which David Hume used, and the logical positivists have added to it the new techniques of linguistics and analysis, displaying a creed of their own. They are metaphysicians of a type presiding over the extension of metaphysics, according to their estimates. That is what they are attempting to do, but they do not seem to realize that scientific theories are not mere transcripts of facts but are interpretations of experience. They look at the world and they try to find out whether this world can be accounted for on the basis of mere chaos or caprice, or whether there is any guiding principle or not.

If you look at the cosmic panorama, the way in which it has developed from matter to life, life to mind, mind to intelligence to spirit, you cannot put it down as merely due to the accident of nature. In other words, you establish that there is an ordering purpose, a guiding intelligence, a cosmic mystery. You may not be able to fathom its nature completely but, all the same, unless you envisage something like that, it will not be possible for you to give an explanation which commends itself to your mind.

And when you talk of experience, it is not something to be limited merely to the experience of space and time. There is intellectual experience, there is moral insight and there is spiritual encounter with the Supreme. The highest kind of experience is one where the human individual is able to feel that he is not a mere fraction of nature, that there is something in him which enables him to sit in judgement on nature, enables him to control nature and thus to escape from the necessities of nature. Unless you regard the individual as a duality of subject and object, as having within himself nature and supernature, it will not be possible for you to account for all the great work which we have done in this world from the time when we were thrust into it down to our present day.

It is essential, therefore, to regard the human individual not as a mere animated instrument, but as someone who is a co-creator with the Divine, who is assisting the purpose of the universe, trying to lead it from one stage to another. Unless we feel that there is such a thing as man's encounter with the Supreme and allow it to constitute an essential element of man's nature, man is not fulfilled, is not complete; he has not reached what he is to reach, unless he is able to develop the spirit in him. We feel that the way in which we give expression to the Supreme, the intellectual ideas, the mental images are relative, transient and should not be taken as final and absolute. Any finality or absolutism in our concept kills spiritual adventure, the process of trying to move forward from stage to stage. Man is here called upon to complete himself. The great tradition of Scottish philosophy, to my mind, is that it is not the positivist emphasis, but the spiritual orientation that all your great theorists have asserted.

What the world requires today is spiritual orientation. We have done so many things in this world, and yet we are afraid of what is likely to happen. That is because man is a duality. He is capable of doing great things and capable of doing very low things. He is at once the scum of creation and the crown of it. This duality, this dichotomy, in his nature has to be overcome. Man must become one, so as to reflect the higher tendencies in him. If he is able to do that, he becomes really what he is intended to become. When that happens, it is what we call the fulfilment of man.

The redemption of the human race as a whole is the goal of human history. That kind of redemption can happen if each individual exerts himself, disciplines himself, puts himself to all sorts of exercises, understands that religion is a costly business. It is not something which we can easily attain, and those who profess to be religious are yet able to tolerate inequity, injustice and terror in the world. It means that some of us who prefer to be religious are tolerating these things.

I only wish to say that when we are in doubt,

the spiritual outlook will give us the courage and the compassion to denounce everything which goes against these fundamentals — the verities of truth, love and goodness.

Address on receiving the Honorary Degree of Laws of the University of Edinburgh, 14 June, 1963.

Greek Thought

You have been working to build up a welfare state in your country based on the great ideals of democracy, freedom and justice, ideals which were first formulated in the West by your spiritual ancestors, the ancient Greeks. Bishop Westcott remarked many decades ago that Greece and India were the most metaphysical nations in the world. It may be true or not, but it is true so far as Greece is concerned.

A metaphysician, very eminent in our own time, passed away a few years ago — Whitehead; he observed that the safest generalization which one could make on the vast European philosophical tradition was to say that it consisted of a series of footnotes to Plato. Plato remains the guide for all the philosophers of the West. In some way the Vedas, including the Upanisads and dialogues of the Buddha, have supplied spiritual nutriment to millions in the East. There is an emphasis, therefore, on metaphysics, on finding out whether this universe has a pattern or not. Man is not merely a tool-maker, he is also a pattern-maker. When he is faced by the things of the world, he wishes to know whether there is any meaning, any principle, underlying this whole cosmic panorama.

The spirit of science which has resulted in such great advances, from steam to electricity, from electricity to atomic power, from atomic power to space travel, has brought the world together and made it a world in which nations and cultures are brought into close intimacy. That was started in the West by the Greek thinkers. I recall that an Egyptian priest told the Greeks, "You Greeks are always young."

There are two types of people in the world: those with ancient traditions looking back to the past with nostalgia, lamenting the loss of a golden age; there are also young people with open minds, with virgin outlook, untrammelled by any kind of pride or prejudice, not oppressed by the weight of antiquity, saying that they look to the future and wish to have a brave new world. The Greeks were the people who said that they were always young, that the universe was rational and could be understood and that we could find out what the truth is. That spirit of science is something which the Greek thinkers contributed to the world of thought. You cannot get a better definition of democracy than what Thucydides gave. Our Constitution is not meant for the few but is meant for the many. Here we do not recognize birth or parentage but the contribution made to the service of the community. That will be the test and we shall try to protect the oppressed and provide equal justice for all.

We do not claim infallibility for ourselves, but we do not admit infallibility in others. You have the fundamental principles of democracy which we are still not able to implement completely in any part of the world. In our own country we have proclaimed these great ideals but we have not been able to translate them into practice completely. We are still far from that goal of a truly democratic society. The spirit of reason and the spirit of democracy are there. But they are not enough.

You find in the world several things, health, beauty and form. They are neutral; they may be used for good purposes or may be turned to evil purposes. Something else, a sense of values, is necessary if society is to be regarded as satisfactory. This sense of values, when we are faced by depression, confusion, fear, anxiety — and these things occur — enables us to turn to the inward sanctuary. That sanctuary is not a place in space, but a state of mind; it is a spiritual consciousness. When we turn to it, we will be able to get some calmness, some composure, some contentment. Without that guiding principle of a divine presence, of a spiritual purpose, it will not be possible for us to make science, democracy and other things function well.

These three great things — the spirit of reason, the spirit of democracy and emphasis on values — are the things that had been adumbrate by the ancient Greek thinkers and we are trying our best to adopt all of them and put them into practice.

Speech at banquet in favour of the King and Queen of Greece at Rashtrapati Bhawan, New Delhi, 2 February, 1963.

India And Nepal : The Heritage

The monarchical tradition in Nepal has been a very long one. The first Lichchhavi King said, "My purified heart tells me that I should work for the good of my people. I am trying my very best to make my people as happy as possible." That is how he put it. He said that the duty of the king was to work for the good of the people over whom he was said to rule. It is that great tradition which Your Majesty has inherited.

Happiness is not something which is merely outward in character. You are paying a visit to Amarnath. When I was in Kathmandu for your coronation, I visited Pasupatinath temple, and I saw the Asokan column on which Asoka, in the 3rd century B.C., inscribed, "Here Buddha, Sakyamuni, was born." Everyone who goes there is impressed by the spirit of religion that prevails in the country, and your intending pilgrimage to Amarnath is an expression of that spirit of the country.

Many of us live on the outward scene; we live from day to day, from hour to hour; there is no pattern, no purpose, there is no studying of our depths, no kindling of the inner light which is there dormant all the time. The Buddhist maxim is: *Om mani padme hum,* the jewel is in the lotus; the Hindu saying is *deho devalayo nama deha,* is the body, the *alaya* of God. So each human being has in him a sacred source of sanctity, a sense of holiness, a spark of divinity, which we in our hectic existence overlook altogether. And that is why we have so many cases of neurosis and instability; there is not that inward anchorage in which alone people can find real comfort.

These great maxims which were announced years ago have not been put into practice by us. They require that we should afford every human being, man or woman, every kind of opportunity to grow into fullness. When we talk about self-expression, we must have a self before we can express it. When we once have a self, all opportunities should be afforded by us by which that self-expression could be realized.

The recent reforms that you have brought about are those asserting the equality of men and women before the law, prohibiting polygamy, encouraging widow-marriages and inter-caste marriage and condemning unequal marriage — we have had terrific instances in our history to show what disastrous results these unequal marriages have had. Take the story of Rama: you know the way in which his father had a queen who wanted her son to be installed on the throne. In spite of all the lessons which our scriptures teach us, we still had a social order which was unequal in character, iniquitous in its nature. These social ills have come down to us from ages past. It requires great courage to scrap them. That you have had the courage to scrap them and introduce a new social code is a matter of gratification to us all. But I should say that inserting anything in a code is different from implementing it. We have inserted in our own code the abolition of untouchability and the repudiation of caste so far as public relations are concerned. But we still know to our cost how these things which obsessed men's minds still have a hold on them. Disciplined effort, education and propaganda are necessary before these laws become actual functioning realities.

Millions of people, everywhere all over the world, are illiterate and submerged in the shadows and they do not lead even a kind of animal existence where they can scrape some food. Such are the intolerable inhuman conditions in which people live in many parts of the world. If we want to remove these evils, it is essential for us to increase our wealth, plan our development, improve our industries and make it possible for our ordinary people to say: we are proud to belong to a country which looks after us, which gives us enough facilities for the expression of our souls.

If social freedom, religious freedom and economic freedom are given to the people, you may take it that they will surmount the tribal loyalties, the smaller group feeling which they have and work for national cohesion. A national consciousness will develop and the individuals will feel that they are effectively participating in the work of the administration, in the work of the government. These things will inevitably follow.

All these things count for nothing unless we preserve peace in this world, unless we have that feeling of *maitri* on which the Buddha insists, the feeling of *sneha,* friendship for all human beings and for all the countries, and understanding of their problems, and not merely sit in judgement on them, trying to find out what their difficulties are. If we are able to get under their skin and find out what their problems are we will have greater understanding of their difficulties and sympathize with them.

The world suffers from lack of communication. If communication is there, not merely the outward communication but the inward communication of heart to heart, or understanding of the problems of other people, this world will become a happier place than what it happens to be at the present moment.

e have so many things in common — a ıon heritage, common aspirations for the e, common ambitions for working for a ›wship of the free nations of the world. The ›eration of fear, so to say, has to be knocked ›wn; a federation of free people will have to be stablished. When we have so many things in common, when we are neighbours ourselves, your security and stability are as vital to us as our security and stability are vital to you. We can, therefore, work with this one common objective of making the people of our countries happier and better than what they happen to be.

Our friendship is based on cultural links, on geographical proximity, on historic traditions, on a great heritage to which we are both heirs. It is my ambition that our policy towards each other must be one, if nothing more, of friendship and the well-being of each other's people.

Speech at dinner in honour of the King and Queen of Nepal, New Delhi, 27 August, 1963.